BLOOD LUST

SCOTT SEDJO

 www.trafford.com

North America & international
toll-free: 1 888 232 4444 (USA & Canada)
fax: 812 355 4082

I

THERE ARE THOSE WHO BELIEVE in the truth of tales of vampires. Of the legends and the folklore, I can say nothing. I am a scientist, and can only speak of that which is based in science. Yet sometimes, perhaps most of the time, folklore is based in science. At any rate, there is a point at which the two intertwine, and become so intermingled that they appear as one. I have had the privilege, to my horror, of witnessing this ghastly metamorphosis, and all the more ghastly, for it was at my own hand. I watched as my experiments took a life of their own. I stood by helplessly as my control dwindled, giving way to chaos, a chaos with its own order and purpose. Perhaps I underestimated the will of life, which sustains it and allows it to thrive in the midst of chaos. But then, I suppose I never really understood, and desired to create something in the midst of nothing.

Some would perhaps call me mad; the ravings of a paranoid culture, fearful of its own shadow. I myself would say I am a misunderstood genius. Yet mad perhaps in seeking not the benefit of a race doomed to destruction. It is not

I but they who hold the seed of their destruction. It is true that I use my talent to further my own power, as do all creatures. Perhaps I helped them with their own demise, perhaps not, I do not know, nor do I care.

Many years ago, when I was still an undergraduate studying biology, I first heard of research being done on genetic cloning. This research immediately sparked my interest, an interest that grew in every fiber of my being. The implications for medical development, in itself, were astounding, not to mention correcting the genetic flaws that humanity had created for itself. It was not I who invented it but I who perfected it. Dolly, the sheep, was already created, yet genetically flawed. I began my experiments. There were immediately laws prohibiting the attempted cloning of human beings. Moralists spouted that it would be unethical, that we would be playing God. What the hell did they think we had been doing for the last ten thousand years, since the agricultural revolution?

We genetically enhance both our animals and pants for our own benefit. We even have methods now to keep alive those that are, by nature, doomed to die; God has nothing to do with it. We even alter our look, enhance our boobs, and change our faces, all the while thumbing our noses at God, as if what He had given us were not enough. I laugh at the impotent notions of their god. I laugh at the sediment that has delegate God to the position of a moralist. I tell you that, from the beginning, God was power. It is the impotence of humanity which found it necessary to assert morality. God kills with impunity, as do we. In this respect, we are gods. We have not yet ascended to the thrown of God, as our power is limited; but we are on our way. The only difference being the confines of our own morality. This moral pedantry was necessary to protect us from those limitations, even from the God whose nature is power. It is for this reason that, within religion, we found it necessary to create a Satan, an embodiment of the power of God that we find distasteful and call evil, to preserve the moral character of God, a character we ourselves impose. This God who commands genocide and had his own son killed must be justified morally; I tell you that God and Satan are the same, and we are He.

After many disappointing trials with only some success, I moved on to 'higher' animals. Yet man, in his exalted status as the pinnacle of evolution, turns out to be far less complex than some of the 'lower' animals. His arrogance, however, reigns supreme, and sickens my soul further as he boasts his superiority. Even among those enlightened minds there remains something of this arrogance; a lingering vestige, I suppose, necessary to be sure of the will to live, to survive, even at the cost of truth. The willful defiance of youth, our beautiful deception hardly proves success. Man has earned some merit, to be sure, a dominance upon the earth for a time. He has yet to prove the test of time. His several million year existence holds nothing compared to the scorpion's 450 million year reign as a top predator of its niche.

I should pity them, I know; yet the more they relish in their own delusion, the greater my scorn became. They attempted to dissuade me, of course, laughed at me and ridiculed me—as the fearful always mock the strong, to save their beloved position. "You cannot possibly clone a human; there are too many factors." The moralist was easier to talk, or, at least, listen, to. At least they were straight with their agenda, unlike the immoralist that stank of morality.

There were indeed unforeseen factors, easily enough overcome, though it did take time. After trial upon trial of primate studies, success! At last, success! I achieved in cloning a baboon. Yet, as is often the case, my success was riddled with setback. I was crushed. My clone was genetically weak—a side effect of the cloning process, I supposed. For weeks I lingered in despair, searching my notes restlessly and going over the autopsy time and again. My clone should have been genetically perfect. I made every calculation and adjustment in the genetic code to ensure it. The autopsy told me as much—perfection, at least in some areas of the body, in others total breakdown. Apparently, the breakdown had been the result of imbalanced genetic material. The discovery was both a joy and a sorrow. For, if the genes altered in the postnatal state, it meant that my clone had been genetically unstable. Yet, it also meant that there could be the possibility of stabilization. The problem, I knew, but how to stabilize an independently growing organism seemed an impassable sorrow. I began to theorize about genetic manipulation, how I might strengthen the gene through manipulation, even inter-species manipulation. Yet I was left with my original problem; I would still need something to act as a stabilizer for the duration of a life.

Suddenly, as if in a dream or lightning or both, it occurred to me that it did not have to be an independent organism; a fact, which was impossible, another fabrication of modernity. Nothing exists in isolation and life must constantly draw on energies outside itself to survive. All living organisms must eat; consume sustenance to sustain life, not to mention the various sources of sustenance food, water, temperature regulation, species propagation. All ultimately derive from our sun, that gigantic dynamo which powers our solar system, including that minuscule and trivial thing called life. Thus reasoning, I undertook study as to how I could use this incredible power to stabilize the genes once they began to grow. I knew that solar cells were being used to create energy and I thought this was a pretty good bet. The energy produced would primarily be in the form of electricity. This, I reasoned, would be perfect for an organism whose nervous system is basically an electric system. While there were indeed changes noted within the neuromuscular juncture, little else was observed. There was no noticeable change to the gene structure; if anything, they lost integrity at an increased rate, most likely due to the increased activity and thus increased energy requirements of the system. Might that be the problem: too much energy? Like a computer simply overloaded by too much power. I was astounded by the thought. Yet the hypothesis was not unsound; it would even be in line with my data. Nature has given us examples of great power produced by low energy models. Infrasound, for instance, has as much, some say more, power as ultrasound at a lower wavelength. Since I fancied nature as my teacher, I decided to put my experiments on photosynthesis aside to explore this new, though unlikely, hypothesis.

How exactly I could do this posed a bit of a problem, at first. But the problem apparently turned out to be no problem at all. As I surmise, the spectrum of energy ran between the organism and the sun, with the sun being the greatest magnitude of energy. Therefore, to decrease the energy would mean to merely move down on the spectrum. But move down to where? I had already dealt with the organism itself and could do no more. Perhaps a nutritive component between the two extremes could provide the necessary balance. But which one; there were so many. In the end, I decided on the shotgun approach; it offered the best odds of success. I could go back later and isolate the exact nutrient, or so I thought.

I needed a constant and fluid compound with as many nutrients as was necessary to sustain life. Once again, nature had already supplied this in the form of blood. My clones, however, already had their own blood. Yet from somewhere in the recesses of my mind I remembered reading of blood doping being used by athletes to enhance performance. If its one group of people who knew about performance, I thought, it would be elite athletes. Athletes stand to make millions of dollars by doing this. It was indeed ironic, I thought with a bitter snicker, how the public will pay them a fortune to perform par excellence, and when they develop a substance that allows that performance, the authorities strip them of their titles and achievements for having an unfair advantage, of cheating. Funny term, cheating, an advantage is neither fair nor unfair; it is simply an advantage.

The idea of infusing a fresh supply of blood was so simple; I was surprised I had not thought of it sooner. I found, however, the blood type necessary for the infusion to be very species specific. For instance, baboons responded specifically to baboon blood and to no other; not even the blood of other primates would suffice. This had the additional and unforeseen advantage, I realized, when I started my human experiments, of making my clones totally dependent on me. Their rationale placed me at the center of their being, and I their source and continued sustenance. This source of control pleased me to no end; I reveled in its implications.

The first human I created, I named Jean, for obvious reasons. There had been experiments before, and improvements after, but Jean was my prototype, my baby. I worked at the time as a phlebotomist where I could easily obtain genetic material. The miniscule amounts I required were not even missed. The material from which I created Jean was of high quality and had come from a woman who was then serving as an assistant professor of research in chemistry.

She was more than I could have hoped for. A bright, lively baby girl; Jean was my pride and my joy. I was as protective as any parent. I supposed that was like it was to be a father. I passed her off as my niece at the few social interactions which we attended. She blended quite well among her peers. Except that Jean was genetically superior to her peers by a factor of two, perhaps three. She grew rapidly, so we never stayed in one place for very long. And as she grew, the frequency with which she needed infusions decreased. The thought that she might outgrow the need for administration altogether struck me as bittersweet. Though I had not anticipated it, it was the perfect way to ensure my control. Yet I was still her father and confident in my ability to maintain control. As rebellious as children can become, they tend to maintain their parents with a certain regard. I felt certain that Jean's superior capacities would only strengthen the bond between us. She developed normally, though much accelerated, and I found, much of my time devoted to her. Other experimentation, for the most part, was put on hold.

For the most part, I taught her myself. She did attend the public school in the area on occasion, mostly for socialization. Socially, she was aloof, but then, so was I. She was a bit confrontational with the other children when she was young. This, at least, I would not have recognized as a problem; yet she was so much stronger than the other children that I feared she might seriously injure one of them. I would often take her aside after one of her scrapes to explain this. I was certain that her superior cognitive abilities would allow her to comprehend this. At any rate, she did outgrow the phase. In fact, she seemed, to a large degree, disinterested in other children and their interests. Perhaps she just outgrew them. Her intellectual capacity grew at a rate which exceeded even her physical development. I schooled her, as best as I could, and, even then I found it a challenge to stay ahead of her. I would often send her to the library to do research or a book report.

I remember like yesterday, waiting for her to return from the library to give her her regular infusion. She must have appeared to be fourteen or fifteen, though chronologically, she was much younger. A strong wind had blown the shutters against the window, and I imagined it was Jean. I looked out the window expecting to see her, but she was not there. I remember hoping she was okay; it was raining pretty hard that November day, the kind of rain that looks miserable from the indoors and is just painful when you are out in it. The time of her arrival came and went. As the minutes passed into hours, I began to panic. I went out to look for her. I went to the library and the librarian told me that she had not seen her since the previous day. My heart sank. I looked at my watch. What could have happened? It had been nearly two hours since her scheduled infusion. Could she even have survived without it? Should I call someone? Who should I call? Who could I call? I could not call the police and tell them of the infusion of which she needed. I could not even explain who she was. For the rest of the day I searched through every back ally and street I could have imagined she might pass. Even into the night and for days afterward, I checked police and hospital records. Checking these records did almost no good, as they were filled with unidentified persons anyway. All it did confirm was that they did not have a dead Jane Doe which I could later put a positive ID to.

A million things rushed thought my head. But through it all, through the sorrow and the fear, there was a greater fear for what had gone wrong with my creation. There were two distinct possibilities: one; she was in a horrible accident; and two, something had gone wrong with her genetic makeup. Of the latter, I could not be certain. Everything had been going so well, for so long. I doubted that it would all just unravel now; yet I had seen it before. Yet the implications to my work . . . Maybe I was too cautious with her. Maybe that was the natural lifespan of what I had created. I did not use her properly in the span that she had. I immediately commenced to clone another. This second clone would have a definite timetable for introduction into society. I decided to make a male this time with an even greater rate of growth.

From the onset, he became an incredibly powerful and talented athlete. Thus, I encouraged him. When I mentioned how much money he could make for me as a prize fighter, he quickly took up pugilism, and I as well, as his manager. His movements were so fluid and graceful; it was amazing watching him in the ring. He learned quickly. Even seasoned trainers commented that he did things in the ring that were not physically possible. He easily won several amateur championships and then turned pro. I always received the lion's share of the purse; even the more because he really did not require money. But it was a shortcoming of modernity which I succumbed. I never cared too much for money, only that I have enough to fund my experiments; but now that I had found a ready means to make a lot of it, I succumbed to the temptations and began to think what I might do with it, though I had no specific agenda. I, of course, convinced myself that I did. It would, after all, fund my projects for a considerable time. My clone stayed with me and trained. Although he really did not require that much training, his superior genetic structure sufficed. Thus I erred in setting these two forces against each other: one of genetic potential, the other of that convention we call money. It is true I earned millions of dollars—or he earned it for me. Yet, I, as the creator, was entitled to all that he had or was. My error was possibly the same error which engulfed boxer ever since they started paying people to fight; I was just surprised to be susceptible to this temptation. I wanted more. Other manager's were afraid to put their fighters in with mine and fights became scarce. I relied on that money to fund my experiments. Thus, I developed a new strategy; one that required my fighter to lose just enough to make him marketable. The strategy worked and we soon got a title shot. The night of the fight, I instructed my fighter to lay low for the first half of the bout, which he did. Unfortunately, he never saw the second. A left uppercut started the final barrage. I never thought he would get caught like that or hurt like that. Two days later, he died of complications sustained by his injuries.

As I cut through the tissue of his chest to perform the autopsy, I found myself thinking of Jean. The clone whose body now lay open before me had not affected me so, even though he died because I told him to. Jean was the first, I lamented. Maybe it was just that I knew what happened with this one, even if I did cause it. At any rate, that was the second time I deviated from my plan, and the second one to wind up dead. But this time, I made a lot of money doing it, and I had something to autopsy at the end. Jean, actually, you could say, did not deviate from the plan. There really was no plan yet. I was still getting the feel of what I could expect. My second clone had already outlived Jean even though he reached maturity in a shorter time. Thus, his productive levels were off the charts as compared with Jean. I still did not know exactly what happened with Jean, whether she died because of some flaw in her genetics or not; but now I could be certain that a flaw had existed.

The results of the autopsy revealed no abnormality or genetic breakdown. Either of which I had expected to see. It was difficult to accept that a creature so superior could lose in such a fashion, and not only lose but be killed. Oh, I had no doubt that my clone could have won had I let him. Still, it proved the control which I possessed over my clones, that they would put themselves in jeopardy, and even die, at a word from me. The instinct for self-preservation did run in these clones, my experience with my second, in the ring, proved that. Actually, I already knew from the fact that they kept coming to me for their infusions. Yet, I did wonder if it was me or the infusions that maintained control. My experiences with number two solidified that it was I.

Through this boxing episode I was able to attain the funds and the resources to fulfill my aspirations. My work had concluded the experimental stage and progressed to the integration stage. Two of my clones were already integrated. Because they were clones, and identical to their host in almost all regard, there was virtually no problem in them assuming the identity of their host. As a bonus, I received a constant supply of fresh blood from those hosts whom I kept chained up in my cellar. I never stopped to consider the moral implications; if I had, I doubted it would have made a difference. I was a scientist; and, like so many scientists, proceed by what is possible according the laws of science, our theories and our data. We are trained in science, not morality. Yet, if I had ever considered that my clones might benefit humanity instead of destroy it; it had long since vanished from my mind.

My clones came back to me three times a day for their infusions, and paid me lavishly. I specifically selected each host from an array of professionals and leaders. My ambitions grew, along with my army of clones. From the police officer who stops you for speeding to the teacher who educates your children, you would never even suspect who might be a clone. Well, almost never. There were occasions, not many, but some, that a spouse or someone close to the host would come to suspect. The suspicion could often be dispelled with assurances from the clone. After all, people often hear what they want to hear and see what they want to see. Some see conspiracy everywhere; it does not exist for others. For those whose suspicions could not be dispelled, however, replacement was a viable option. It was a bit of a lengthy process, and, therefore, undesirable. The clone could always stall long enough for us to get our pieces into place, if necessary.

Nothing could stop me now. The world was mine for the taking. Yet, in the midst of my triumph, I began to second guess myself. While waiting for my clones one spring morning, I began to prepare their infusions and felt as if someone was watching me from behind. "You're early," I said, looking at my watch and then finishing the preparations. Turning with the hypo, I noticed no one there. My mind was playing tricks on me, I chuckled. Ten minutes later, they arrived. I administered the infusions, and nothing more happed that day that was odd. Yet my thoughts seemed to dwell on that one oddity, as if it really was that odd. I dismissed it as overwork and thought nothing more about it. It happened several more times over the next several days. Convinced it was some small thing brought on by the stress of my work, I determined not to let it turn into a big one. I had, after all, already achieved more than I could have imagined. Perhaps world domination could wait. Then I began to think that which no scientist should ever think, and to ask what no scientist should ask: WHY? Why did I need, or want, world domination?

It was a perfect autumn morning as I went down to the creek behind the house, as I always did these days. The sunshine glistened off the dewy leaves that had fallen in previous day. When I got to the creek, I noticed a young woman standing in almost the exact spot which I usually sat. I hesitated and then approached, "Lovely day," I said. She turned toward me and faintly smiled. She was lovely and seemed somehow familiar. I had seen her seductively inquisitive glances around town before but I did not know who she was. "Yes," she said, turning her gaze back to the creek. I sat down and she sat beside me. We spoke little and mostly just enjoyed each other's company.

She was there the next day, and the next. On the third day, I began to wonder, "Why does a beautiful young lady come down here every morning to sit with an old guy like me?" I was not that old, though considerably older than she. She looked at me as though surprised, "It's so peaceful down here," and she looked back toward the creek. "The waters calm my soul." After hesitating, she began again, cautiously, as though unsure she should speak any more, "My father used to bring me down here when I was very small." I looked at her hard; and she looked at me, her face erupting into a soft smile. "Father."

"Jean?" I inquire, in disbelief. It had been nearly fifteen years since I had seen her. Could it be? All of my other clones were dead. My first, the only one I actually named—was it possible? "How can this be?"

She told me over the next hours and days of her life that nearly ended, of her struggles to survive. "The evening I last saw you, the eve of the accident, I walked to the library as usual. But instead of going in, I stood outside, staring, wondering why I was there. I knew I was studying, and I knew you wanted me to study, but I didn't know if I wanted to study. Not that I didn't, it just had never occurred to me that I could choose not to study if I wanted. You would still be there for me. I walked for some time and found myself at the park. I sat and read for a while until it began to get dark, then I headed to the library. It got dark and cold really quickly, and began to rain. I decided to return home. It was almost time for my infusion, anyway." I cringed at the thought of that chilly night. "Several blocks from home I heard a screech and a crash. I saw the car that hit me and then I woke up in the hospital. They said I should have died, perhaps I did die. But the transfusion they gave me helped me regain my strength. Anyway, I remembered what you had said about not letting anyone find out what I am, so I left. However, it occurred to me that the hospital had given me my infusion, not you. I was no longer bound to you for that reason, and decided to conduct my own experiment as to how far I could go. I could always give myself an infusion; I knew how. But I didn't think you would approve, so I left. I went south. The first injections that I gave myself consisted of blood gathered from the various vagrants with whom I associated. The quality of blood was low, and I could tell; like the engine of a car, I suppose, it sustained me but little else."

"I found that by drinking the blood instead of injecting it, my body's own filtration system could filter out the impurities and purify the nutrients that I needed. It took some getting used to, both psychologically and physiologically. I could barely get myself to drink it at first. I kept telling myself it was just an experiment, like you had taught me. Still, after the first few drops I thought I would puke, and I injected the rest. About a half hour later, however, I felt rejuvenated, like the times right after you had given me infusions. I surmised that it took some time for the nutrients to get through my system. After that, my body began to crave it. I still had some aversion to drinking blood, but it quickly subsided as my body's cravings grew. I taught myself to hunt and thrilled in its embrace. It gave me new purpose even if it was only temporary. I wondered if the filtration of my body could overcome the problem you dealt with: that of interspecies blood. The blood should, after all, contain the same basic nutrients. Yet, for some reason, it did not work. I forced myself to drink a sizable quantity of it; nothing happened, other than it turned my stomach. That was a bit strange that it should turn my stomach when I was already partially accustomed to drinking human blood. It really doesn't matter why, but I guess my body just craved human blood; other species' blood simply did not have the necessary components."

"After I got to the city, there was no problem finding blood. I worked as a prostitute," she went on as though it was nothing, but I cringed, "giving men what they wanted and taking what I needed. Some of them died; some did not. With a plentiful supply of blood, I grew powerful. Yet, I would look up at the stars in the sky, the way we used to and wonder what you were doing. I guess I never imagined that you would continue your experiments after me." She stopped abruptly and looked at me with piercing eyes.

"How did you know?" I inquired, since I did not make my experiments known.

"I know," she said, averting her glance, "I have watched you for some time now." I looked at her in shock. The thought of being watched was disquieting, and a bit creepy. It had been years since I had conducted any of that work, and my clones were all dead. "No," she looked at me and smiled an amused and whimsical smile. "They are the reason I am here. They are mine now, numbers four, five, and six, as you call them. You created them and left them to die, but I taught them to hunt; to survive."

"They did not take to the idea of hunting nearly as well as I," she continued. "Funny," she said in a kind of ironic manner, "for all their intellect, they seemed to have a real difficulty associating hunting with surviving. Whether it was an inability to see hunting as necessary, or some moral vestige that they may have had, I do not know. All I know is that it took a considerable amount of energy on my part, and only three were able to adapt. They did learn to hunt very well and very quickly. Yet, even after they knew how to hunt, they seemed to lack the will, or the desire, to hunt." I could see that she was visibly perplexed, and could tell that it disturbed her all the more that she had picked up hunting so naturally, almost instinctively, and no one had taught her.

I was dumbfounded. Could what she said be true? Could my clones still be alive, after all this time? "How is that possible? I had always assumed the span of life to be much lower and my research indicated as much."

"Obviously, you were mistaken," she said, trying not to mock me. "Your clones, though inferior to me, are also strengthened by the hunt. It challenges them to survive and makes them strong."

It was the first time I realized she did not think of herself as one of my clones. I suppose she was right. I did not even think of her like that, but more like my child. I had asked nothing of her and given her my own lifeblood in return. "So, you know my work and you control my clones; why have you now returned to me?"

"I want something," she said, "I want your research," but her eyes revealed that she wanted more than my research—much more. Besides, she already knew what my research contained. I looked at her inquisitively and began to speak, yet thought the futility of it and headed to the cellar to retrieve my papers. She followed. Handing the volumes of notes to her, she glanced briefly at one or two. "This is all trivial to me," she said, putting the papers on the table and looking at me with that slightly seductive look I had seen when I first saw her down by the creek.

"I thought it would be," I said, "You already know it. So, I ask you again, what do you want?"

"Don't you see," she said with a coy smile, "I am your research and I have surpassed your research." She turned to face the wall for a moment, "Give me an honest answer," she implored, and turned back to face me, "Why did you create me?"

I thought of all the times she had asked that same question when she was a child. I thought of my answer. And I knew it would not suffice now. "I created you for the betterment of humanity."

She was silent but her eyes cut through my soul as if they were knives. "I asked you to be honest," she said in a very quiet and disappointed voice, as though I, like others, might not even know my own lies. "You care as little about humanity as I." She repeated her question, this time, more forcefully.

"Because I could," I said, knowing no answer would suffice, and hoping a non-answer would. Her expression was blank and dispassionate; but I could tell that it did suffice. "So what will you do now?" I asked.

"I will do what I have always done," she said in a somewhat tired voice, "what all creatures do—survive."

"Is that what you came for?" I asked, assuming that it was, and assuring her that I enjoyed seeing her. I did enjoy seeing her; she was, after all, my daughter. It was just incredibly overwhelming: a daughter I had not seen in fifteen years and presumed dead, a life that I had not led in over five, and creatures that I created to live only at my side, apparently thriving without me.

"Partially," she said, and flashed her seductively sly grin, "the rest will have to wait till tomorrow. It's late and you're tired." Before I could ask her where she was going, she was gone. Out for a midnight stroll, I presumed. I dared not to think of anything more. I knew I would not be able to sleep and lounged by the television to get my mind on something else. Yet my mind lingered, trying to digest the events of that day. Would she return? What more could she want? Maybe it was sediment for her father; maybe it was . . . I dared not think it. It really did not matter now.

I awoke on the sofa, a news program on the TV in front of me. Had I been awake about an hour earlier, I would have seen the story of the two murders, each within two blocks of me, and would have immediately been suspicious. As it was, I was glad for the events of the previous day, and found myself hoping for my daughter's return. I lumbered to the kitchen to make my yogurt smoothie, as I always had for breakfast. Seated at the table, drinking a smoothie of her own, was Jean, in a very revealing dark green night gown and nothing else. I remember how the gown accentuated the dark red highlights of her hair, and wondered why I should notice that. "Yours is on the counter," she said, looking straight at me to see if I would say anything.

"Jean!" I cried, in surprise, "what are you doing?"

"Getting breakfast," she replied, gulping hers down. I could not figure out if I was happy to see her or not. I suppose I was, but at the same time, felt very vulnerable. "I spent the night last night," she stated, "is that okay?" The latter part obviously added to maintain pleasantries; it was clear that she was not asking permission and turned squarely toward me. Her night clothes were ever more revealing than I had realized. I told her my robe was upstairs. "I know," she said, squaring up to me again. "I know the ways of men," and left to get the robe. While she was gone, I took the opportunity to examine the glass she had prepared for me. It looked and smelled alright. It tasted fine and I drink it.

When she returned, she was dressed. I looked at her; there were so many things I wanted to know. Maybe now she would tell me what she wanted. "You are my creator," she said, leading be back to the sofa. Her touch was warm and soft, much softer than it had been before. "I want you," she said, abruptly, almost as if she could not express her whole thought and had to rely on a prearranged script. "What do you mean?" I asked in astonishment. She explained to me her life of the past fifteen years, living in shadows, as she put it. And that she did not want to remain in the shadows. "I am the first and the last of my kind. I am alone."

"Didn't you say that the others survived?" I interrupted.

"Yes; they had, and had grown strong, stronger, at least. Since I taught them of the hunt, it encompasses them; they are little else. They don't mind the shadows. I do. They know nothing else, nor do they want anything else. If I had not taught them to hunt, they would have meagerly extinguished. My experiences at such a young age imprinted on me the will to survive. They did not have that, and haven't the capacity for any will that is not generated by another. I do. I want to step out of those shadows and make my mark in eternity."

I struggled to even comprehend what she was telling me. "I want a child, someone like me," she continued, "but you know this is impossible; as your own research indicates, we, I, am infertile." The need to propagate the species, I had never imagined she would feel it; so much the more, I supposed, for being the only one of her kind (though I wondered at the differences of the others.) I had added slight genetic alterations between Jean and my second clone. I supposed that the acceleration of growth patterns would have invariable lead to the loss of some other trait. Jean called this trait the Will. And one facet of the Will is to propagate the species; there are over seven billion people in the world, so most people barely notice it; yet magnify that urge by seven billion, and that would be what I imagined Jean must be feeling.

"What can I do?" I asked with genuine sympathy. I did not know if I could do anything to help, or even if I wanted to. Not because I had no feeling for her, but because I did not know whether it would be a good idea. Perhaps I had become a bit more reflective with age; perhaps I was just justifying my own retirement. "Help me to create again, not like the others, but someone like me."

"I'm retired," I replied without hesitation "You have the research. You don't need me."

She looked at me as though she already knew all that, and could have taken it if she had so desired.

"Then allow me to conduct the procedure here." Her request was quite unanticipated and a lot to ask. I did not know whether I could have another creation take place in my home, under my roof, and not be part of it. But I did not want to be part of it, especially the creation of one like

Jean. Jean was special, and I loved her. Yet if I had known of the emotional bond that would develop between us, I never would have created her. I was not sure if I wanted to go through it again, rather, I was sure that I did not.

"Why here; you already have the research?" I inquire; trying to say that I did not want her here without saying 'no.'

"You have the materials and the necessary supplies right here. Besides, I have nowhere else to work." She replied, and assured me that I need not have anything to do with the experiments. After much discussion on the matter, and against my better judgment, she wore me down and I relented. Strange, I thought, that I cared what she thought of me, and strange too was the fact that I should not be able to tell her 'no.' This was a fact that she knew and relied upon.

Jean commenced with her experiments the next day. I barely saw her at all for the rest of the week; this was my intension, and Jean understood. The first day, when I went down to show her the notes and get things going was hard. It was even more difficult to leave the cellar and do nothing; so I avoided her. After a while, I was fine. The cellar was so removed from the rest of the house that I barely noticed. I began to think that maybe it was not a mistake. I began to entertain thoughts that I never had before. Good thoughts. When Jean was successful, we would all be sort of like a family, I smiled an amused smile; a strange family, but a family.

Yet, I began to hear things, strange things. At first they were merely creaking noises in the walls or something easily dismissed. I will be the first to admit that it was probable that I was somewhat paranoid at this point. Years of secrecy tend to take their toll on one's psyche. Yet then it was the whispers, inaudible mumblings in the dark, always in the dark. I casually asked Jean if she had had anyone over, to help her or otherwise. She denied having done so, and I just figured I was hearing things. Still, it did begin when Jean moved in and began her work. Maybe there was a connection. Maybe my subconscious was trying to tell me something. I was sure that was it: my subconscious was trying to tell me that it was not a good idea to allow Jean to conduct her experiments in my home. This, I already knew. I had an uneasy feeling about it; so what? The die had been cast and the game must be played. The only thing to do was to do the best I could with the hand I had been dealt.

Rumors began to circulate about strange goings on concerning my house; rumors that I would have found disturbing had I heard any of them. As it was, I did not get out much, and even when I did I seldom took the time to listen to anybody. Yet, the sounds I was hearing in the night did make it increasingly difficult to sleep. This further added to my paranoia, until one night I was sure I heard a knock at the door. I was in bed and would have waited for them to go away, but the knock grew progressively louder. Somewhat annoyed, I forced myself out of bed and put my bathrobe on. When I opened the door, there was no one there. The last knock was not more than two seconds previous, but there was no sign of anybody. I wondered where Jean was as I closed and locked the door. I went down to the cellar; Jean was not there, but her experiment was. I looked in awe at the sight before me. There on the table were six mug sized test tubes, each of which contained a human fetus. As I marveled that I had done nothing so sophisticated, I realized that she was not producing one child, but a whole army. To what end I could only imagine . . .

"What are you doing?" I turned to see Jean crouching at the bottom of the stairs, as if ready to spring; her lips red with blood and her eyes locked on me.

"I just heard a knock at the door," I said, trying to pull the situation away form the present moment, "I was wondering if you heard it?"

"Yes," she said, not unaware of what I was attempting, "I heard it; and I took care of it." She looked at me again and, deciding I was no threat, asked what I thought of her progress. Instantaneously and yet in slow motion, I watched as she transformed from some ravenous wolverine-woman into the sophisticated and somewhat seductive young woman I knew as Jean. Her eyes softened, she straightened to full height, threw out her chest and wiped the blood from her mouth, all in one motion; except her eyes did not really soften, instead they went from crazy eyes filled with bloodlust to steely and reserved, and they locked onto me as if a self-guided missile.

"Pretty elaborate," I said, as Jean began to approach me scraping her nails along the concrete wall as she came. They left their mark, and the sound they made as they did so pierced the core of my being. It was then I knew how razor sharp and strong those claws really were, claws I had admired from afar as elaborate fingernails of painted beauty. It was clear now that they were also formidable weapons. "How many are you making?" I asked.

"One," she replied, still making her way toward me, as if that was what I wanted to hear. "You know how many trials it takes to get just one right." She stopped upon reaching the table, and, inspecting her creation as if to see if anything had been disturbed, she diverted her gaze from me. I did know how many trials it took to get just one right, and I knew that this was not how it was done.

"Jean," I implored in defeat, "I don't know if I can have this done here."

"Where else would I go?" she said, anticipating my question and still looking at the jars, "I'm almost finished."

I did not sleep much over the next several nights. I was plagued with the image of the clone I had created. It was not Jean; it was the wolverine-woman crouching at the bottom of the stairs, with blood on her lips. How many victims had she taken, I wondered. A rhetorical question, I supposed. I had not created her for that; I was not sure anymore why I created her, but, at this moment, I was sure it was not for that. It was true that I had done things, perhaps comparable to what Jean was now doing but to watch it going on is a different matter. I knew now what I must do. It began with me and it must end with me. I grabbed a knife from the kitchen and went down to the cellar. The jars were on the table, with the fetuses inside. In fact it looked exactly as it had before, no new growth, no anything, and I wondered if it was a different batch altogether. I opened one and gripped the knife, raising it. My arm seared in pain and I spun as I dropped the knife. The jar crashed to the floor as the wolverine-woman shoved me into the wall with such force that my nose erupted with blood. I looked at her, and she transformed as she had before. "Father!" she said, trying to contain her fury, "I have tried to be patient with you!" She stood there eying me with her steel eyes, though I could see the bloodlust behind them that she would not allow out. I crouched in the corner holding my arm; if the wrist was not broken, it was damaged and useless.

"I could help you," I cried, attempting to render a compromise, "I could help you create one!"

"No! she said, forcefully but calmly, "You already had that chance and declined it." She looked at the contents of the jar that had shattered on the floor and then at the knife lying beside it, then at me, my face smeared with blood. "Did you think that this was my only facet? Did you think that if you destroyed these, I had no more?" she asked sounding very disappointed. "Father, you underestimate me." I implored her again to help her and about the other fetuses to which she referred. She looked at me and smiled, "I don't need your help. And of the others, I do not tell you to protect you. If I did tell you, and something went wrong, or if you did something stupid, like right now, I would have to kill you."

Well, I thought, at least I knew that it was not her intension to kill me, and I knew that what she protected was far more valuable to her than these. I pulled myself up, still grasping my arm and took a step toward her, "What will you do, now?" she laughed as she stepped toward me; I had not seen her laugh like that since she was a girl. "I will do as all creatures do, as I have always done—survive."

When I revived she was gone, her work was gone, everything was gone, and I was weak for loss of blood. And the only thing that remained to tell me that she was ever there was my broken wrist.

Watching the news, drink in hand, I was struck by the number of disappearances that there had been. I could not say whether Jean was involved, but every time I heard of a disappearance or a homicide, I thought of her and her brood and wondered. I should have seen the signs: Jean's wanting a child, her change in behavior, her jars of fetuses, and then her statement indicating that they were not so important; and then, looking back in hindsight, her appearance. Jean was pregnant. I could only suppose that if she had managed that, that she had been successful, if not, she would try again until she was. From what I saw, she could have a whole litter of children by now. There were also the others—the clones that I had created—to help her. One way or another, she would create an army, a race of . . . people that needed human blood to survive. And, like her, they would not be content to live in the shadows. There would be war, and wars to come. It was inevitable when two species compete for the same resource, of this I was sure. I went over to the window and looked out at the neighborhood. Maybe it would not come for a couple decades, but it would come. And when it did, I would watch dispassionately and know that it began with me.

II

THE STORY OF JEAN

THE FIRST MEMORY I HAVE of my life is gazing up at the stars with my father. It was a warm summer night and the stars shone especially brilliantly. I am not sure where we lived at that time, since we tended to move a lot. It must have been after one of my injections because I was upset and he was trying to comfort me. I was often upset by my injections when I was young. I must have only been two or three; at least, that was what I thought at the time. He pointed out different stars and constellations. There were so many and each one had a name. I wanted to know all of them. "That one up there," he said, trying to trace the stars, "that is Sagittarius, the hunter; that is the sign that you were born under." I remember being really confused by this, until my father explained that the stars moved, and what he meant by 'under' was actually 'aligned.' Then I looked at wonder in the general direction of Sagittarius, wonder that I was aligned with a hunter in the stars. Later, I discovered that my father had been looking at me with the same wonder.

My father told me on numerous occasions how special I was. He said that I was superior to other children. I never understood just what he meant until one day at recess when I was skipping rope, some of the older girls came over and told me, in a not at all friendly way, that they were going to skip now and needed my rope. This was odd, I thought, but since the rope was not mine to begin with, I gave it to them. I picked up a ball and began to bounce it against the wall. Several minutes later, one of the girls informed me that it was her ball. I started to leave along the blacktop, and another one informed me that they needed it for cheerleading practice, and I would have to go somewhere else. When I pointed out that there were other people on the field, the girl just seemed to get upset at me. She wanted to teach me a lesson. I was not quite sure what she meant by that; usually I liked learning lessons, but something about her tone told me I would not like this one. One of the other girls interrupted her, "No; I'm sure she's got some great dance moves. Let her show some to us."

"Well, alright." I had been practicing some tai chi moves that my father had taught me, and proceeded to execute them.

"What's she doing?" one of the girls exclaimed, holding back laughter. "I don't know," said another, bursting into laughter, "but it's not dancing." A third held me back, "No, no, no; try this." I watched as she did her little dance with twirls and flips and such. I had seen nothing like it before, it did have a certain dynamic quality that I found appealing, though I doubted it had much, if any, practical value. I was pretty good at mimicking, in fact, that was primarily the way my father taught me. I immediately began to mimic the steps I was shown, perfectly, I thought. Then, the laughter stopped and one of the girls grabbed me again; this time much harder. She pushed me to the ground "Try this," she began her dance again, but this time, instead of kicking the air, her kick landed squarely on my face, sending me sprawling to the ground. "Oh! I'm so sorry," she exclaimed, putting her hands over her mouth to cover a delighted smile. I just looked at her; maybe it did have practical vale after all. "You gonna cry?" one of the girl asked, mockingly. Why would I do that, I wondered, and started to walk away. I had never felt this kind of mocking hostility before. "Where you going?" one of the girls asked, as she grabbed me and tossed me to another. Evidently they were not done with me yet, but I was done with them. So when the third came to launch a punch to my midsection, I turned my grip on the one that was holding my arms and used her body to beat my assailant to the ground. The third girl, who had been standing by, then rushed me, after I discarded her friend. Her rush would have been easily avoided, but instead, I grabbed her, lifting her high into the air and threw her. She landed hard about several yards behind me. I looked at her lying on the ground, her face and matted hair smeared with a mixture of mud and blood; I looked at them all as if I could not believe what I had done. Not that I did not know I was capable; my father had always told me what I was capable of, I guess he was right. I just never thought it would be necessary.

The next day, we moved again; and my father had a long talk with me again about how I was genetically superior to others, and about how I could not let anyone know I was different. He told me I must take extra care not to injure anyone because of my superior strength. I tried to explain that I was not the one who picked the fight, but he did not listen. He did not seem angry, but, whether he believed me or not did not matter; what mattered was what I had done and that someone may have been seriously hurt as a result. I had known what I was, since I was small, my father had explained to me that he created me by manipulating genes in a laboratory, which was, in fact, how I got my name; that that was why I needed injections three times a day. I did not want to hurt anyone; yet I remembered how I felt during that incident, not anger but more of a burning inside me; and I knew that I could not ever let anyone treat me like that.

My father chose to school me at home so I did not get to enroll at the new school. I guess it was just as well; standard curriculum always seemed to move too slowly for me, and I really enjoyed being taught by my father. He was so smart; he was, after all, a scientist. He created me, how many other fathers can say that? Not in the primal, biological, luck-of-the-draw and chaotic sort of way, but through a calculated, scientific and selective process. Sometimes, I ask him why he created me; he would usually smile, draw me close and hug me, something he rarely did. Then he would tell me that he created me genetically perfect because of humanities imperfections, because they were frail and weak and would eventually destroy themselves. I do not think that, at the time, either of us knew the implications or the reality of what he said. At the time, it made me feel special and loved, and that was enough.

My studies went well enough; I especially liked our field excursions. I am not sure how my father obtained a passport for me since I was living 'under the radar' as he put it, but he got the papers for us to explore around the Mediterranean. First on our itinerary would be Egypt, followed by Turkey, the Greek Islands, and then mainland Greece. We explored the pyramids of Egypt, and my father challenged me on just how they could build them over 4000 years ago with copper tools when our biggest cranes today would have a most difficult time even moving the 50 ton stones. I looked at him and then ran my hand over the bottom stone of the great pyramid in wonder. It was the oldest of the seven wonders; now it was the only one still standing. A fraction of its former glory, we could not destroy it much less duplicate it. The invasions of the first millennium proved that. "How was it created, father?" I asked, turning an inquisitive graze on him. He looked up at its majesty, at the alabaster-coated top were the invaders could not reach, "*dia tos theos,*" he said, in reverence, and in an ancient form of Attic, a dialect of Greek. I looked up, "with the gods," I whispered, and knew it to be true. "People have only a superficial grasp of time," he turned his gaze toward me. "They suppose that proving one thing necessarily negate others."

After the pyramids of Giza, we hired a car to take us down to Luxor, the ancient capital of Thebes and the Valley of Kings by way of Abydos. Abydos was small and rural, like many Egyptian villages. And, like many villages, the Nile bestowed its life in a series of inlets and canals. Unlike many villages its history was sacred, and had been for thousands of years before the pharaohs; so much so that Sety I, after his father founded the 19th dynasty, built a temple there to honor the site. This temple holds the listing of names, in Egyptian hieroglyphs, called cartouches, of the rulers of

Egypt. It is by this cartouche list that archaeologists derive much of their knowledge. Yet the list does have notable exceptions. The pharaoh queen, Hatshepsut, was stricken from the record when her son ascended the thrown. Women had been able to serve as regents, and even to act as queens; but to acquire the power and majesty of a pharaoh—the world would not be ready for that for at least another millennium—when another Egyptian, Cleopatra, ascended the thrown.

Yet Sety built his monument, his temple, in honor of a monument that had already existed for over a thousand years. A temple far below the desert because of its age and now threatened as the rising waters of the Nile extended their reach. This is the Osireion, amply named, for it is here that the head of the god Osiris is said to be buried. And the waters now rising are considered sacred and magical. They contained the magic of Isis, the wife and sister of Osiris, magic she used to restore Osiris after his brother, Set, murdered him to attain the thrown.

Osiris is said to have first unified upper and lower Egypt, and Egypt prospered. Upon his murder, and subsequent dismemberment, his body parts were scattered along the Nile. The reign of Set was short and turbulent, filled with darkness. But Isis collected the pieces of her husband, and used her magic to restore him to life. She had a son by him who would avenge his father and take the thrown. Osiris now rules as lord of the dead, just as his son rules as lord of the living.

Looking into the waters the now filled the Osireion, I felt an instant and powerful connection with its god. Maybe it was because I too had been reconstructed from a variety of parts, at least, that was what it felt like. But, then again, maybe, just maybe, I was the usurper.

It was hot the day we walked in the Valley of Kings, and the sun beat down unrelentingly on us. The desert landscape was filled with the heads of tombs, tombs that extended far beneath the earth and consisted of a variety of chambers. Better to be below ground, in the tombs, where the sun did not reach. It was a different world underground, strangely eerie, this land of death, yet full of reverence and wonder at the promise of new life. To the east, stood the magnificent temple of Karnack, with its sphinxes and pools inside. What caught my attention were the obelisks, glorious monuments to the reign of the pharaoh-queen. They were, indeed, towering structures, pointed toward the sky and the power of heaven. They were simple structures, like the Washington Monument, but all the more impressive and powerful for being built out of a single block of granite weighing tens of thousands of pounds. Even its discoloration, an attempt by her descendants to erase her name and inscription, could do nothing to discredit the magnificence of the structure. I wondered why they had left the obelisks intact. Perhaps they knew that history could not be stopped; it could only be rewritten.

Unfortunately, our Mediterranean tour was cut short, and we had to return home without visiting Greece or Turkey. It was a shame; I was so looking forward to exploring Crete and the ruins of Minos. I am not exactly sure why we had to go back early. My father said it had something to do with my infusions but did not elaborate. He seldom discussed my infusions with me. I knew that they were blood infusions, but next to nothing about their preparation. I could not imagine it would be that difficult or force us to alter our plans.

Returning to the States, I concluded my studies of the Middle East at our local library. I found that actually being there had given me a whole new perspective on a subject I thought I knew. I often pondered this dichotomy on my walks to and from the library. Not that I did not enjoy my studies, I relished them; yet they paled in comparison with knowledge that came from actual experience. On one such occasion, I simply walked right by the library, wondering what experience might have in store for me. Before long a storm blew in, and a pretty bad one at that. I decided to go back. Soon it had gotten so dark and rainy that visibility was impaired. There was a screech and then a thud and I turned just in time to see the headlights.

I woke in the hospital with an IV in my arm and a bandage on my head. I watched as the IV dripped its contents into me. I looked at the clock; it had been hours since the scheduled infusion that I never got. I looked back at the IV; but I did get my infusion, I thought, just not from my father. My father! He would be very angry if these hospital people found out that I was not exactly human. At this point I may not have been thinking too clearly. I was human, even if I was a clone, and my motivation for doing what I did would have been the same. And I had never seen my father get 'very angry' in my whole life, I had no reason to think that he would start now.

I pulled the IV from my arm, found some clothes, and started walking.

Over the hill, I could see our little house in the distance, and then I stopped. It was everything I knew, yet the world had so much more. My father was there, my creator, who loved me, yet, I did not know his reasoning, but I knew there were things of my creation that he was not telling me, perhaps of my potential. I did love him; yet the hospital had given me my infusion, not him. And, if the hospital gave me my infusion, I reasoned, then so could I. I turned toward the horizon; the first rays of sunlight had just begun to peek through the dense and rolling expanse of clouds. It called to me, as Isis called to Osiris, and I knew it was time for me to go. With a deep breath, I started walking, to see what the world had to offer, to see what I really could do. I found myself walking toward the bus station and went inside. I would have just enough money to make it to Houston. I stopped before I bought the ticket. The trip would take nearly a day and I had not even worked out how to do my infusions yet. Well, I thought, leaving the station, at least now I knew what I had to figure out first. I thought about it a lot, as I was walking, becoming a bit anxious over it; I was already beginning to feel the effects. I needed an infusion and I needed it fast. But how would I . . . I need not have been so anxious; when the time came, I took what I needed. Everything seemed to become fuzzy, everything except the blood that I required. I was walking through one of the seedier parts of town, whether by design or whether I just stumbled there, I do not know. But when I felt the burn so intensely that I could not go on, I fell on a man who looked like he was sleeping on a bench. I plunged the needle into his arm and pulled out a syringe of fresh blood. The man stirred but he did not wake. I injected myself and quickly left, hoping no one had seen me. I felt the color come back to my face and the awareness of my surroundings revive. It was like waking from a dream, I had only a vague notion of how I had gotten there. I began to look for landmarks which might indicate where I was, all the while thinking that I really should not let myself go so long without an infusion.

My next infusion was a little more precarious, the woman whom I had set upon woke up after I drew her blood. A sharp blow to the base of the head put her back to sleep and there were no further problems. And, so I lived this way, drifting from town to town. Still, I worried about the quality of blood that I got from my donors. Somehow it was inferior to those which my father administered; worse yet, what if I got some type of disease. Yet, the answer, I pondered, might lie in the folklore of the vampire. That, to which I refer, also has a basis in the natural world. Vampire bats and leeches also subsist on blood of others; yet they ingest it. Perhaps the natural process of digestion could act as a kind of filter, after all, that was its basic function. I decided to try it on my next donor. After drawing the blood, I left to find a secluded spot where I could work. I went down to the river that ran through town and sat down on the bench. I had always liked watching running water and fondly remembered how my father and I would frequent such places. I poured the syringe of blood into a plastic cup that I had gotten the night before and brought it to my lips. One quick gulp and it would be gone. Yet, I stopped; I was not sure why I stopped. The putrid smell of blood was only that: a smell. Yet the more I hesitated, the more revolted I became. Quick, Jean, I kept telling myself, before it starts to coagulate. I poured it down, and gaged in convulsion as my gulp became a sip. My hand dropped and I returned the majority of the fluid to the syringe, and injected it.

I sat gazing at the syringe and then out at the flowing water of the river, water always seemed to soothe me. My father and I would often walk down to the banks of streams, brooks or rivers; sometimes I would play by the waters edge, sometimes we would talk, often we would just sit and listen to the flow of the water. Right now, I needed to hear the soothing sounds of the water. Why had it been so hard for me to drink blood? I pondered. Hunters did it, I knew, some sort of ritual about drinking the blood of your first kill. And I was a scientist, at least, the daughter of one. It did not smell, or even taste, that bad. Still, I was physically revolted; probably psychological, I thought, a vestige of the moral pedantry given to me by my father. The thought made me laugh. It was mildly amusing; still the problem remained: what do I do about it?

I need not have worried. Within about half an hour, I started to feel better and stronger than I had in a long time. I actually felt, or thought I felt, the blood coursing through my veins. Nature, it seemed, had figured out my problem for me. I was no longer revolted by blood. Their blood was my blood; I just had to take it. I became a huntress. The prospects of the hunt thrilled me; and I found even more ingenious and profitable ways to hunt. Men were easy targets. I did not need to find them; they found me, and they paid me for it. Most found my lust for blood kinky, and let me proceed. Of course, I gave them the sex they had come for, and there were no problems. Occasionally, however, there was a problem. The guy would find my bloodlust repulsive and refuse to give me any, often I could convince him by succumbing to an unusual erotic fantasy of his. If that did not work, he either paid me but I left without my feeding, or I took what I needed by force, depending on how close I was to my scheduled feeding. Soon I had enough money for a car of my own and could drive to Houston.

"Marie Jensen," I heard from the blue station wagon pulling up beside me, "is that you?" I glanced at the car to be sure that the question had been directed toward me. "I'm whoever you want me to be," I said in my seductive working voice. The passenger door flung opened, and I got in. "I never thought to see you here," the man said as he drove. "Are you alright?"

"Of course," I replied. "Are you looking for a good time?"

The man eyed me eerily, as if realizing his mistake, "You are Marie; aren't you?"

"Sure, baby," I replied, not letting on that I was becoming a bit uncomfortable. I was this far, I figured; I was in this guy's car and it was close to my feeding time. I could not afford to let this one go, no matter who he thought I was.

"You're not in town for the convention," he said, looking for a place to let me out, and told me I looked exactly like someone he knew, while hiding his embarrassment behind a feeble smile. I replied that I was not but asked if he could take me to the bus station. Of course, he agreed, against his better judgment, and I proceeded to tell him about how I needed money to get home, and that was the only reason I was out that night. I told him I lived in Dallas when he asked me, and he said that he might be able to help me out. I looked at him trying to discern what he meant. I hoped he did not intend to give me the money and let me out at the bus station. He turned the car onto an abandon dirt road not far from the station. "Maybe there is something you can do," he said, stopping the car and looking straight ahead. He unzipped his pants, grabbed the back of my neck, and forced my head into his lap. I bit down hard. He screamed in pain and disbelief at seeing his lap fill with his own blood. I sat up fast, so as not to give him time to strike or grab my head, and, in the same motion, drove my claws up through the bottom of his jaw. The sight of so much blood was both exhilarating and revolting. Yet, it was my sustenance, and, therefore, it could not be repulsive. I gorged myself with as much blood as I could, slicing the flesh off the corpse in the process. Once the bloodlust had left me, I sat mesmerized by the bloody mess that was before me. I was drenched in blood and felt an urgent need to get away. Yet, how could I get away? Surely, I would leave a trace. I could not think of that now. I opened the car door, making sure to smudge any of the blood-soaked fingerprints I left behind. I ran off the dirt road and out into the night. The swamps were not far, and I headed that way.

I ran through the night. I ran, and the dawn came. Maybe it was farther than I thought. I should have taken the car, I thought, as I ran. I was hot and thirsty and my feet hurt. My high-healed boots had been discarded long ago; and my feet, I am sure, were bruised and blistered. I did not look down to see; I needed to get as much distance before the authorities started to track me, if they had not already. I could barely see the sun rise, and what I could was painful. The provocative make-up that is the trademark of every whore now streamed down my face in clumps mixed with sweat. Though the majority of it had slid off my face, enough was left in my eyes that it left me half blind. Only a whisper of a thought crossed my mind about my next feeding. Had I been aware of the thought, I might have been anxious that it was overdue. As it was, I supposed that my previous gorging meal sufficed, and thought nothing more about it. I had no time to think; I ran. My eyes and lungs burned; and still, I ran. My feet felt the shock of every rock they stumbled upon; and still, I ran. I ran well into the morning until I could run no more. I stumbled and fell. The dust of the earth stuck to my sweaty body as I rolled on the ground. I wiped the sweat from my eyes, or tried to, and rolled on my back to see the sun high in the sky. This was it, I thought. This was my choice. I could lay down now and die or I could get up and run. Survival called to me, the Will for survival; Osiris, torn to pieces and reborn. I pulled myself up, and my Will made me run. Each step was painful; but the pain only confirmed that I was alive. I went numb and was, most likely, delirious; but suddenly, out of nowhere, there was a pond or a lake in front of me. I ran faster, as if pulled magnetically, and jumped in. The water was a shock and soothing at the same time. I opened my mouth and let the cool liquid flow in. Only after I had washed my grimy face and could see again, did I realize how uncomfortable my tight corset had been. It probably did not help much for running, I mused ironically, and removed it. Only when I threw the corset up on shore, did I see the children playing down the beach. Without knowing why, I began swimming toward them, and, suddenly, I realize how hungry I was.

There was a man on the shore with a small child, evidently the father, and three children playing at the water's edge. Evidently, the man had seen me, because he made a motion to the children, and they left. As I was all alone, I decided to take a bath, and removed my other garments. By this time, however, all that was left was the short miniskirt I was wearing. It was tight and not at all comfortable to run in, but the tear I had made in it did allow enough movement to run. I did not realize just how uncomfortable it was until I removed it and threw it on the bank with my corset. It was such a relief to be free of the constricting whore clothing. I sank into the cool waters, letting them soothe my stiff and aching body. A short time later, I noticed a man walking down to the water's edge. He seemed to be coming right for me, and I wondered if it was the same man I saw earlier. As he walked toward me, I swam toward him. He walked straight into the waters and was looking straight at me, at my nakedness beneath the waters. Evidently, he was stalking me; so much the better. "Join me," I enticed, with my most provocative smile, trying to hide the bloodlust that threatened to erupt inside me. He gazed at my breasts, floating in the water as I swam, as if the desire of he eyes could pull back the waters. I stopped and jumped, as if to make them more appealing. I burned, but I waited. The weakness and fatigue of my body was replaced by intense anticipation. All the fibers in my being were coiled and ready to spring. Closer and closer he came toward me. Hotter and hotter I burned. He grabbed me with the force of his lust as he came near. I let out a squeal as I felt him thrust his hard member into me from beneath the waters. The squeal I released contained the lust of my soul, and my burning broke forth. I grabbed the sides of his head, tearing flesh from his neck. He began to scream, but I jumped on him, letting his warm blood flow into my desirous mouth, in the process, forcing him under the now bloody water. A moment later, we reemerged. He was now still, his neck broken, as his blood dripped from the sides of my mouth. I looked about; and, seeing no one, I brought him to the bank to feed.

There was no time to rest. I was not sure whether the authorities were on my trail; or, if so, how far behind they were. I decided to swim up river. Swimming naked might be fine, but I would need something to wear when I got out of the river. I looked at my corset and skirt on the bank, and swam over to retrieve them. I picked them up and hesitated. Examining the garments for a moment, I took the money out of my corset that I had stuffed there the previous day and threw the clothes into the water, and swam over to where I had left the corps. Floating near it were his denim shorts. I put them on, and then retrieved his t-shirt from the bank were he had left it. The clothes were a bit big on me, but they would do. Actually, I much preferred clothes that were too big to my tight whore clothes; at least, they let you breathe. It was too bad I could not take the shoes lying beside the shirt; my feet would really be hurting once I started walking again. I swam, trying to consider my options of where to go next. I probably should leave, of that I was certain; but I was not sure whether I could even risk going back to retrieve my stuff. Right now, I swam; there would be plenty of time to consider my options later. By dusk I had decided to at least go back and try to get my car. I emerged from the water and looked back over the darkening sky. Perhaps that was not such a good idea, I thought; I had run probably over twelve hours the previous night. I had no wish to repeat it; besides, my feet would never agree to it. They were bruised, scraped, blistered and shoeless. I walked in the shallows following the river, to try not to be too hard on them. Late that night, I came across a road that crossed the river and turned onto it. Soon there were signs of a town up ahead. I had no sooner seen these signs than a white sports car pulled up beside me. The man inside offered me a ride into town. "No," I said, but somehow it came out "yes," and I got in. I really did not want to kill anyone tonight. But, I needed to eat; once again, the will to survive dictates. There were two other men with the driver and I became nervous. They were a bit rambunctious, as well as intoxicated, and I knew what they wanted. I suggested they stop at a motel, I pleaded. The driver turned off the road and then turned toward me. He told me that there was nothing they could do in a motel that they could not do in a car. The one beside me in the backseat, who had been fondling my hair and then my breasts, reached over to kiss me. I was too weak and weary to fight. I let them take me, one after another after another, and sometimes all at once; all the time, I was growing weaker. At last, it was over, after what seemed like hours. Two of them were in the car; the third was passed out on top of me on the ground outside. I quickly sliced his neck open and took what I needed. His blood drained neatly into my mouth. I stopped short of my fill this time so the man would not die, and covered the wound to stop the bleeding. When his friends came out to get him, they stopped at the sight of the blood that had fallen on the ground. I convinced them that the blood was mine, that their passed-out friend had been a little too vigorous. They loaded him into the car and gave me a ride into town. The driver apologized as he let me out of the car. I laughed out loud at the futility and stupidity of an apology, but not until they drove away.

I checked into a motel for the night. After a hot bath and a good night's sleep, I decided to look up this Anne Jensen, or whatever her name was, that caused all this trouble. It was just a mistaken identity that that guy in Huston mistook me for. But maybe, just maybe, it was more than that. I proceeded on my hunch and got on the internet down at the local library. I was in luck, on my first search I found her, but her name was not Anne, it was Marie. Evidently, she had written several articles on biochemistry and had just come out with her second book on the subject. I checked the catalogue for any editions of her first book they might have, and proceeded to the shelves to find it. Turning immediately to the back cover, I was astonished and delighted by what I saw. My hunch had been correct; it was me. At least, the picture on the back cover looked exactly like me. I had suspected as much, and more. I suspected that we not only shared the same features, but the same genes. My father had told me enough about my creation to know that there should be someone out there with the same genes as mine. My genetic material was derived from another; not in the usual way, where genetic material derived from a mother and father combine to produce a wholly unique expression. I was a clone, and exact replica of another's genetic material; I was, therefore, literally and genetically, another Marie Jensen, and Marie Jensen lived in California.

I went, as fast as I could to the bus station. I was determined to find this other me, as I fondly named her, but first, I would need to get my car. The ride was not that long, and I mused how much more comfortable and efficient it was than running. I did look briefly for any news about the murder, and found nothing; which did not mean there was nothing, only that I did not find it. It was nice to have my car again and some good clean clothes. I headed out leisurely to California; since I would still have to stop to hunt, I did not want to take a too direct route, besides, I was in no hurry. I usually found what I needed along the way, someone willing to trade sex for blood; and, as in Houston, I was usually paid for it. Usually my donor was male but occasionally female. I preferred male blood, which was a bit interesting, considering I was female. Trading for blood meant two things: it meant that I did not drink my whole fill and the donor lived; and it meant that I would have to feed more often. Still, this was preferable. I did not want to kill anyone unless I had to. Entering into a state of bloodlust made that almost impossible. I became powerfully driven toward one objective: at the same time, because all my energy was focused on that one goal, everything else seemed to fade into the background. Though I found the feeling of power I experienced in a state of bloodlust most exhilarating, I did not care much for the loss of control which accompanied it. I eventually made it to my destination and began to look up Jensen in the phonebook. It seemed there were quite a few Jensens, but not one Marie Jensen, or even M Jensen. This is where the work began, I mused. The thought briefly occurred to me that Marie Jensen may be unlisted; after all, if she was some type of celebrity, she may not want people to be able to look her up in a phonebook. This was indeed a lengthy and tedious process; looking up names, calling people to see if they had any information on Marie. Yet I was able to use the time to think and ponder what I might do if, or when, I found her. I did not even know what to say when I found her. You do not exactly walk up to someone and say that you are their clone.

After some time, I called a Paul Jensen who told me that Marie was his wife. He told me that she was at the research institute working now but he would be happy to take a message. I said I would call back. I had a lead, and decided to go down to the institute to follow up. I still was not sure how to introduce myself, if it was her. Just seeing someone who looked exactly like her might freak her out. Maybe I should just wait in the parking lot, I thought, as I drove up, I turned the ignition off, and realized that I was not even sure if this was the right research institute. Surely, if she worked there, her name would be on the directory in the lobby. I went in; sure enough, there it was: Marie Jensen, Ph.D., 5th floor. I went back to the car. I waited there for some time, pondering how to proceed. And as I pondered, Marie walked out of the building. It was an eerie feeling watching someone who looked exactly like me. Of course, she wore her hair differently and wore glasses, most likely due to some genetic weakness, a weakness of which I did not share. She started her car and pulled out of the parking lot. I followed. I could take her place, I though; after all, was that not what my father had intended? He never told me in so many words, but I could surmise as much from the fact that he wanted to create genetically perfect individuals who looked exactly like their host. I could be all wrong. I had no idea whether he created any other clones. I had never seen any of his work and, to my knowledge, he discontinued it after me. But, I knew that was his original plan, at least. Once he had told me that there would be others; several times he had spoken of me as being the first among many. I followed Marie to her house, but kept driving, as she pulled in. I needed more information before I made my next move.

The following day, I called Marie at work. "Marie Jensen. You don't know me, but my name is Jean. I need to talk with you about some of your work in genetic engineering," I stammered.

"Jean?" she asked, totally off-guard. "What about my work in genetics?"

"Specifically, about the possibilities for genetic cloning. I was hoping I could meet with you to discuss it."

"You could come by my office, if you'd like," she suggested.

"I thought we might meet for lunch or something," I countered, thinking it might not be such a good idea to go to her office. I could tell she was intrigued; I just did not know whether she was intrigued enough to meet with me on my terms.

"Well," she debated, "I am going on lunch pretty soon. Maybe I could meet you for lunch."

"Great." We made plans to meet at a diner down the street from where Marie worked.

"Oh, one more thing," I added, "don't be shocked if I look quite a bit like you." Now, she was really intrigued, I thought as I hung up the phone; but better she be shocked now than at the restaurant.

I arrived at the diner early. I thought it would be better if she approached me rather than I her. Marie arrived about ten minutes later. Her eye widened as she saw me, and she hurried over to my booth. I was not at all sure she would not run when she saw me, and was glad to see her approach. "Jean?" she asked, with a smile of bewilderment. "It's like looking in a mirror." I greeted her and motioned for her to sit. Our waitress came over and Marie ordered a coffee and a sandwich as the waitress refilled my coffee cup. "You said you looked like me," Marie said, looking at me, still bewildered, and pouring the packet of sugar-substitute into her coffee, "but I had no idea . . ." she trailed off. "No wonder you didn't want to come to my office."

She suspected, as I thought she might, but would not come out and say it; nor would I, not yet. We chatted about meaningless things, about work, about family, and about genetics and chemistry, carefully avoiding all conversation that might be a little too in-depth. Marie said she enjoyed meeting with me, as she grabbed for the bill that had been placed on our table. I told her that I had more to tell her but it needed to be a little more private, as I grabbed the bill away from her. She looked at me inquisitively, as if surprised, or maybe, as if she had suspected the surprise. We made plans to meet again the following day, this time, at a park not far from where Marie worked. As she rose to leave, I added that there was one more thing. She glanced at me inquisitively again. I asked her not to reveal to anyone about our meetings. She smiled and nodded faintly, as if she understood, and I joined her as she walked out.

The next day, we met and strolled in the park down the jogging trail, adjacent to the pond. After a time, we stopped to sit on a bench, shaded by trees and overlooking the pond. I looked deeply toward the pond, its still waters glimmering in the sunlight. "Your suspicions about me are correct," I said suddenly, without changing my gaze. "I am a clone," I stated, turning toward her to see her reaction. Marie remained calm and, for a time, did not look at me.

Eventually, she turned her gaze toward me. It was a blank gaze, not inquisitive like before; and I explained how I was created and how I came to seek her out. "That explains it," she said, with almost no feeling in her voice. She inquired about my father, and whether he had published any of his work.

"Not to my knowledge," I explained. I did not think she believed me, and, maybe worse, she might think that I was crazy. Not that I cared much about what she thought, but, I had learned long ago to care about what other people could do with their knowledge. She might just avoid me for the rest of her life, which would be fine. But, she could go to the authorities, thinking I am some dangerous stalker. I cursed myself for revealing so much. Father was right; I could not reveal myself to anyone. I knew what I had to do; and, as Marie rose to leave, I did it. I launched my frame directly at her and, with a quick turn, snapped her neck. I hoped she had felt no pain, and sat her back down to cradle her head in my arms. I fed on the corpse, and then went to get a blanket from her—my—car. I was Marie Jensen now. I rolled her in the blanket and put her in the car, and then left for work. I said I was not feeling well and took the rest of the day off. I went to Marie's home. If I was Marie now, I had a husband, and he was home right now. I knew from talking with Marie, that Paul worked nights, but not much more. He was sleeping when I got home, which gave me a chance to look for any clues that might tell me something about him or about my life there. He was surprised to see me at home as he woke. I told him I was not feeling well, so he said we could go out to dinner that night. Evidently, we were in the habit of having dinner at home before he went to work. I made a note of it. After dinner, he left for work and said I should get some sleep. He kissed me goodbye and I watched him go. After and hour or so, I took the shovel from the garage, and the body of Marie from my car, and buried her in the garden in the backyard.

My new life did have certain advantages. I had a steady job and income. And, of course, since I was a creation of genetic engineering, I found research in the field quite fascinating. I could finally conduct my research as to the particular nutrient in human blood which I needed to sustain my life. My job at the genetic institute did afford me an ample supply of blood and I had no need to hunt, spending more time in research. Yet I found myself, on more than one occasion, contemplating the wisdom of my research. Strange, I thought, remembering how vile I found my first hunt and taste of blood, how foreign that feeling was to me now. Even though "hunting" for me was essentially "trading," I still felt the thrill of finding the blood I required in a living human being. The taste too of stored blood paled in caparison to fresh. I speculated that it had superior nutritive qualities, though I suspected my preference merely psychological. The compulsion to hunt had been ingrained in me; it was part of me now. I could not give it up totally, and I failed to see why I should try. I limited myself to hunting one or two times a week.

My husband was probably the nicest benefit of my new life. For the first time in my life, since I was with my father, I had a sense of belonging. I also had an identity which afforded me more access to travel, which David and I did frequently. Our favorite place was Cancun, although he enjoyed it more than I. Just having him around was nice, even though we really did not see each other that much. Maybe it was precisely because we did not see each other that much that we got along so well, at least, I with him. I dared not tell him much about me after my encounter with his wife. I did not want to have to kill him like I killed Marie. Yet, in the back of my mind, I knew I would, eventually. And, the uneasy thought left me somewhat reserved when I was with him. But, I had learned how to be whatever, or whoever, a man might want me to be; and, for now, I was Marie.

My life took another turn that September when Paul switched to the day shift. I was a bit apprehensive about spending more time with him, and even more apprehensive when he said we would now be able to have the family that I always wanted. I attempted a smile, but it hardly covered my bewilderment. I had not foreseen that Marie would want a baby; and, I guess I should have. It really should have been anticipated; the drive to reproduce is biologically programed into the female of the species. It is just a matter of time as to how and when that programming expresses itself. This new development, however, presented some difficulty. As a clone, I was unable to conceive or become pregnant; at least, that was what my father told me. I had never questioned him on this nor had I looked into the matter; but I had the equipment at work and determined to do so. My tests were extensive and a bit unpleasant since I was female, but did verify my father's statement. My sex chromosomes were not developed in the proper way for coupling; rather, I had a full assortment of chromosomes in my cells as opposed to the half necessary for sexual reproduction. However, the cells were distinct in nature in that they were immature cells and theoretically capable of replication. This prospect intrigued me; I was not biologically equipped for sexual reproduction, but maybe I was equipped for asexual reproduction. Yet, now was not the time to allow my fancy to wander. It did not help me with my currant problem. Even if I had a child, it would be a clone of me. (A clone of a clone; another note to consider later.) Perhaps a clone would do, yet that would mean telling Paul things that might be best unsaid, and that might lead to his death.

Over the next few weeks Paul and I tried desperately to have a baby, which was a little annoying. Other than that, it was kind of like one of our vacations, and we got along better than I expected. There were adjustments to be made, of course, few of which were actually addressed in a productive manner; and, as the weeks wore on, these issues erupted into points of aggravation. My inability to conceive, along with my late nights at work began to raise suspicions from my husband. I resisted his suggestions that we see a fertility specialist for as long as I could. Finally, I said I would ask my doctor about it, and gave Paul a medical excuse for my inability to conceive. I thought this would suffice and that would be the end of it. I was wrong. It now became a problem that he had to fix. He wanted more counseling and more tests; obviously there was something we could do, he reasoned. I suggested we wait for the moment; maybe a baby just was not in our plans right now. Things returned to normal for about a week. Then, one night, after I got home late, he told me that he had been hearing rumors about me. Then, he came right out and said it; he accused me of having an affair and that was the reason I did not want to have his baby. His argument was so absurd, it was almost comical. Yet I knew where he got his accusations. I looked at him, and, for a moment thought of telling him that I had been out, drinking other men's blood, and wondered what he would do. I walked slowly to the window, and, looking out asked, "What if I was?" He told me he would divorce me, his voice trembling with rage and fear. I tuned toward him; his words were more of an idle threat than a promise. I looked at him with compassion; here was a man, trying desperately to salvage something that I just wanted to get rid of. Still, divorce would be preferable to killing him; and I would get to keep my identity, something I had not had until I met Paul. Yet, now I knew, for what he was concerned, I was having an affair. I all but admitted it, and there was no point in denying it now. "Maybe we should take some time apart," I suggested. Paul was shocked and hurt by the suggestion, and did not know how to respond. He grabbed a blanket and went downstairs to sleep on the sofa. I watched him go, in his little tiff, and wondered why people ever got married in the first place.

It was nice to just lie alone on the bed and think. I had not even considered divorce a viable option until Paul brought it up; and, at the moment, it seemed my best option. Paul was upset, and I was sorry about that. But I did not see myself continuing in the marriage. I had always assumed that, sooner or later, I would end up killing him. But the one thing I treasured from the marriage—an identity—I was fairly certain I would lose if I killed him. The next day, we barely spoke; and the day after that, and the day after that. When I did bring up the subject, he avoided it by pretending to be involved in something important and saying that we would talk later. Later never came. Finally I told him that if there was something more important than our marriage, he needed to take care of it without me, and that I would be gone the following day. Apparently, I had miscalculated the meaning of his silence; I should have just left. He looked at me but his look was not the pleading, helpless look I had anticipated; instead, it was a glare full of rage, rage that I did not know Paul was capable of; but, it was the rage all creatures are capable of when they have been hurt. "So, that's it," he said in an ominously soft voice. He stepped toward me, "You whore!" he yelled suddenly, and raised his hand as if to hit me. I do not know if he would have; but, at that moment, my own instincts kicked in. I grabbed his raised arm and flung him across the room, still in control of my faculties enough to know that I did not want to kill him. I could not kill him, if I did, all would be lost. He broke through the closet door as he landed. He rose in surprise, "Is this what you want!" he yelled, as if debating whether to rush me or to give up his position. I had hoped he would choose the latter. I knew I could easily avoid his rush; but, if he persisted in his attack, I could not be sure what I might do. I was wrong again, and it was beginning to annoy me. I saw him raise the revolver; presumably he had picked it up from the closet he had broken into, or maybe it had been in his pocket. I do not know, nor it did it make any difference. Looking back, I do not think he would have fired on his own; I forced him to it. I leapt toward him in a zigzag motion and grabbed the gun. As I did, he fired, grazing my neck. Blood had been spilt, my blood. I tore the gun from his hand and threw him with such force that he nearly broke through a wall this time. I leapt toward him and grabbed his neck before he fell. He took a half-hearted swing at me. I swung him around and choked the life out of him. I fed, and then dug up his wife and placed her beside him. Maybe the authorities would think they killed each other; at any rate, they would not be looking for someone who looks exactly like the wife. Marie's corpse was not in too bad of shape. I should be able to get some distance from the house before anyone could determine that she had already been dead for some time.

Dragging the body into place, I stopped to examine the scene, and, with a deep and regretful breath, thought of all the things I had just lost. I would turn back to my life in the shadows, alone with no identity. I took some money and some jewelry and got in my car, the one I had when I first met Marie. I had kept it for such an occasion as this, but, somehow, I had wished it would never come. It was Jean's car, and Jean was nobody. I put the key in the ignition, hoping it would start after all this time. After the third try, it finally started and I was off. Again, I had no destination, and again just to get distance from where I was; and again, I was Jean. I made it to Nevada before I let myself even ponder of a destination or what I should do next. I kept thinking of Paul's proposal to have a child. It would not have worked, not the way he intended anyway. Yet the notion was appealing, after all, I was the only one of my kind; and, suddenly, I felt painfully alone. Maybe, I thought, I should go back to see my father. He was not like me, but he knew what I was; after all, he did create me. I knew it would not be the same; he did not have the control over me that he once had, and I doubted that he would accept my hunting. Perhaps I could go back and just see what he was up to and whether he had continued his research. Who knows, I thought hopefully, there may be more like me after all.

I had to resist the urge to run to my father the first time I saw him. I was not at all sure how he would greet me.

Yet my heart leapt when I saw him, and I wondered why I left in the first place. Of course, I knew, I could not have stayed. I watched him for the remainder of the day, in his laboratory. It looked like he was going over his notes and testing different specimens under the microscope. I was glad to see him still working on his research. It probably meant that he had more clones, I speculated. As evening approached, I noticed two men approached my father. One was tall and thin appearing to be in his mid-thirties; the other was shorter and more portly and appeared to be around fifty. Both men were well-dressed in business attire; and, something about the way they moved struck me. Their strides seemed to be just a little too long for the height of each man and the legs seemed to bend a little too much. The swing of their arms also seemed somewhat exaggerated. At first I thought it was just my imagination, and then I noticed what my father was doing at his table. He was preparing two hypos. It had been a while since I had had an infusion, but it was unmistakable; these were the same type of infusions he had given to me. These were his clones coming to get their scheduled infusions! I watched as my father administered each infusion in turn. After each infusion, I saw the recipient pay my father money, then turn to leave. There was no small talk, no talk at all. I was not sure what I expected, but, surely, it was more than this. He was their creator, their father; this was no more than a business relationship. He had never treated me that way. I decided to follow the clones to see where they lived. It turned out they lived only a half a block away and right next door to each other. I made a note of it and returned to my father's laboratory. He was not there so I crept in to take a look at his notes; what I saw astonished me. I picked up his notebook but, before I got a chance to look through it, I noticed another book full of newspaper clippings. The first clipping I read was about a professional boxer who had died after a championship match and my father's picture was in the paper. He had been the fighter's manager. It was not hard to put two and two together, and, reading through the notebook confirmed my suspicions: the boxer, Max, was one of my father's clones, although he never mentioned his name. The clone was referred to as number two. Evidently it was his first clone after me. I did not know how a genetically superior clone could die in a boxing match with a human being, nor did I know if my father had not been exploiting his clone.

I watched my father over the next several months as his cliental of clones came to him for their regular infusions. After the clones had left and my father retired for the evening, I would often examine his research. I could find no traces of any new research. He was not attempting to isolate the nutrient in blood that the clones required, nor was he creating any more clones. It appeared his work had stagnated. He was preparing and injecting the infusions, but nothing more. It was like a business; I suppose it was his business, perhaps a perfect business. He created the clones to be dependent on him, and then they paid him for that which they required. I could not blame my father, after all, why should he not be paid by what he created? At the same time, I could identify with his clones; I was, after all, one of them. This is what I had yearned for, to have others like me, to not be so alone anymore. The infusions were not necessary; I could teach them to hunt for themselves. I had learned, and I did not even have anyone to teach me.

The next day, I met the man named Jack. It was so much easier for me to meet a clone than a human being. I simply showed up at his doorstep. "Number four, I presume?" I asked with a hopeful smile. Instantly, he knew that I knew what he was. I was a bit surprised by his warm greeting. He seemed to lack all suspicion. He invited me inside and offered me a drink, which I declined. Since he already knew that I knew what he was, I got right to the point. "The infusions that Dr. Brodiv has been giving you are unnecessary." He looked at me inquisitively, but did not seem surprised. I explained that I was a clone too, the first clone Dr. Brodiv ever created, and that I no longer relied on infusions. I told him how I leaned to hunt and offered to teach him.

"Why would I want to do that?" Jack asked, perplexed. "I was incorporated here with a good job and a beautiful wife. Dr. Brodiv supplies what I need. Why should I change that?"

Jack's statements caught me off-guard. I had anticipated that it might be difficult to convince him to hunt; but, after talking with him, I found myself asking why I should. Jack had a good life here, a life here that was not confined to shadows, which was more than I could say. There was no reason for him to change it. We talked a little more about my father and his research. I asked how many others there were. I was shocked to find that, not only did Jack not know, but he seemed totally unconcerned about the whole matter. The only other clone he knew by name was his neighbor, Bob. I thanked him for his time, and, before I left, I asked him not to tell Dr. Brodiv that he had seen me. I hesitated, waiting for Jack to ask me "why not;" he never did. He agreed, and I left; that was all.

The next day, I met with Bob. He was more open to the possibility of hunting, possibly due to his younger age. The idea of hunting was intriguing, yet the moral implications of hunting humans posed a problem for him. I understood; they had posed the same problem for me. I had had no choice; they did. It was similar with all the clones I visited, and I found myself asking whether I would have started hunting if I had not had to in order to survive. I remember how revolting it was the first time and how difficult it had been to get the first few drops down, and my answer was "no." Yet I could not go back. I was stronger for the hunt; and I was dependent on no one. As appealing as those qualities may be, they are not necessary. I was not like them; I sighed, and needed not make them like me.

Some of the younger clones were a little more adventurous and began to experiment in drinking blood. It was usually a drop or two from a consenting individual, usually a friend or spouse. They always returned to the infusions. Yet the seed had been planted, they knew that they could do this if they had to. Soon, they did.

I observed the number of clones that came for their infusions decline rapidly over the next several days; and after a week, only Jack came to visit him. Soon that stopped. Apparently, when some of the clones experimented with hunting, they did not take too well. Two went rogue and ended up in jail. One was killed; and all of them disrupted their feeding schedules. This is what happened to the one that died; he disrupted his schedule to the point that his body became emaciated for lack of blood. I think he was the only one to experience the actual bloodlust that I experience after I go too long without feeding. He did not really know how to hunt; apparently, he went crazy on a street outside of a shopping mall and started chasing people with a knife. He was shot by police. There was nothing on the news to link my father to the incident, yet it provoked him to withdraw from administering infusions altogether. I saw Jack after they stopped; he basically just lay down and died. I pleaded with him to hunt. I would even get the blood for him. Even offered with necessity, he refused to hunt; I was at a loss. He just had no Will to survive, which is the only way I can explain it. I tried to show the others how to hunt. Although they never really caught on very well, at least, they were willing to learn. I suspected that the ability to learn might have to do with age. Jack, although he was created after me, and was, chronologically younger, his aging was accelerated to the point that he was biologically at least ten years my elder.

The younger ones were able to adapt fairly well. Yet even those that were strong enough to survive seemed to lack a certain quality. Perhaps, because I had to teach them to hunt at a later stage in life, they lacked the proper instinct. They became preoccupied with where they would get their next meal and it left little time for anything else. I waited for them to grow out of it, as I thought they might, but I waited in vain. Not a single clone grew out of that preoccupation, not even the younger ones. Observing this, my heart sank, I knew that they were not like me and never could be. I longed for someone like me; and I knew that path would lead me to confront my father. I longed to see him again and to talk with him; yet I was afraid of what I might have to do should he refuse me. If his reception of the other clones was any indication, he would not receive me well. But I was not like his other clones, I was Jean, and we had had some wonderful times, the two of us. I wondered if those memories were true, whether it was all an act on my account; he was after all, a scientist and I his experiment.

Over the next two weeks, I familiarized myself with my father's itinerary. He was retired now, and I would have expected that he would change his schedule from day to day. Yet his schedule remained very much regimented; he was, like the rest of his race, a creature of habit. Every morning, he rose early to watch the sunrise, then he read his newspaper, had his coffee and usually a breakfast shake that he made himself. A little after eight, he went down to the river where he used to take me, and sat for about an hour. I often wondered what he was thinking and imagined it was of days gone past. He would walk slowly home for lunch and then do some reading or watch television. Between four and five, he went down to the sports bar, which he co-owned, and spent the evening going over paperwork, eating, drinking, and watching boxing on the television. He stayed until close, and then went home to plop into bed and do it all again the next day.

I was at the river before he got there. I noticed that it was too low for this time of year; its waters had slowed to a crawl. Still, it was comforting to see after all these years, and I walked along its banks remembering good times that had been and imagining what might be to come. He was my father, my creator; nothing could change that. My very existence I owed to him, and I would die rather than hurt him. I looked deep into the water and smiled at the irony. I saw the image of the man I had drowned so long ago. I was not at all confident that my words were true. I came to the place where he usually went, where the trees broke to let the sunshine in. There was a bench and one standing rock, perfect for sitting and viewing the river, or just warming oneself in the sun. I glanced at my watch; it was still early and he had not yet arrived. The golden sunlight was breaking through the trees and glistening on the water. I had a feeling it would be a good day. He arrived shortly thereafter; I smiled and nodded. He returned them and said something about it being a nice day, small talk to make sure I would accept his presence rather than saying anything important about that particular day. I agreed, and he sat down on the bench; I on the rock. He stayed for his usual hour and, though I could surmise that he was curious about just who I was and why I was there, we did not speak. The next days were the same. I just gave him a chance to get used to my presence, nothing more.

On the third day, he spoke. "Why does a lovely young lady come down here every morning to sit with an old guy like me?" he asked, whimsically.

I smiled; he was not that old, and told him that the waters soothed my soul. Looking out into the flowing waters I told him of how my father used to bring me down to the river to calm me. I glanced at him and saw the recognition in his eyes. They were filled with an almost wonder and disbelief, the kind of disbelief one experiences when something is too good to be true, and are then afraid to hope but cannot resist for the temptation. "Father," I said softly, looking straight at him.

"Jean?!" he cried back, in wonderful disbelief.

III

EPILOGUE

BRODIV SAT IN HIS TAVERN, switching his glance from the television screen to the beer he was nursing and back again. It had begun to snow outside, and Brodiv could imagine Jean peering in through the window. Everything seemed to remind him of her these days, not the wolverine seductress she had become, but the sweet girl he had once loved and called daughter. Perhaps his love for her had changed him in ways that he did not fully understand. In a way, she, what she became, fulfilled the path on which he had been; namely, a path of destruction, in which he sought to replace the human race. Maybe it was his loss of control over that replacement that he found so distasteful, but he no longer desired it. Now he was just tired; and the future would unravel without him. Another held the keys to the future, and he was sure that other was Jean. She would carry on the replacement which he had begun but no longer wanted; and she would do it in a much more forceful and violent way than he had ever imagined. Yet, if he had to pass on the keys to the future, he was, in a way, glad that they passed to Jean and no other.

Jean had three offspring that year and nursed them with the blood of men. Three more followed the year after that and they grew strong. She knew as well as Brodiv that conflict was inevitable; it was just a matter of time. War was coming. She would, one day take her brood from the shadows. They would walk proudly and take their rightful place in the next stage of evolution. It was inevitable; but for now, she and her brood would live among the shadows. For now, they would be content to wait.